The Adventures of Zelda:
The One and Only Pug

The Adventures of Zelda:
The One and Only Pug

Kristen Otte

The Adventures of Zelda: The One and Only Pug

First Print Edition: 2016

Editor: Candace Johnson
Cover Design: Michael McFarland

ISBN: 1530456622
ISBN-13: 978-1530456628

This book is dedicated to the jelly bean.

Table of Contents

Chapter 1
The Creek

The car veers to the right and shifts to a slow speed. I rise from Ben's lap in the backseat of the car and look out the window. Ahead of the car, I see a large group of trees. The tops of the never-ending tall trees sway with the breeze. Peach groans from her seat in Hannah's lap in the front of the car. I ignore her and turn to gaze at the trees. A blur of brown moves from branch to branch.

Is that a squirrel?

I press my face to the glass to get a better look. The car comes to a stop, and my face bangs against the glass. *Ow.* I take a step backward.

"I have Zelda," Ben says. With my leash in his hand, he opens the door. I jump to the ground and take a look around me. A few cars are lined up next to each other. In front of the rows of cars, I see an open field of grass. I pull Ben in that direction.

"Hold on," he says.

I hear the jingle of Peach's collar. She jumps from the car. Nate holds her leash. I pull a second time in the direction of the grass. Ben follows my lead this time.

The grass is tall, rising to my head. I sneeze three times from the tickle of the grass against my nose.

"Ben, the creek is this way," Hannah says. I look back at my family. Peach is leading our family in the opposite direction across the parking lot.

Wait a minute! I can't be last!

I engage my pug super speed and sprint forward, dragging Ben with me.

As we catch up to the others, the parking lot ends, turning into a small patch of grass. Beyond the grass are the tall trees. The trees diverge from each other to create a dirt path. Peach and I lead the way on the path. The path reeks of interesting smells. Peach and I run from one side of the path to the other to investigate everything.

A rustle in the trees diverts my attention from below. I look up to see a squirrel standing above me.

Is that Squeaks? No, it couldn't be.

I take a few steps to one side so I'm not directly underneath the squirrel. I don't want any acorns to drop on my head.

Peach reacts in the opposite manner. She jumps and leaps at the tree. It looks like she is trying to climb the tree. *Silly Peach.*

The path winds up a hill and then starts a descent. The sound of wind echoes, but I don't feel a breeze in my fur. As we follow the trail down a steep dirt path, the sound grows louder. I stop and step on the edge of the path, looking below us. The sound isn't wind. It is water! A small trail of water moves on the ground below us. I lick my lips.

"Come on, Zelda. The creek is down the path." Ben tugs on the leash. I glance ahead. The path leads right to the edge of the water. Peach is ahead of me again. I hurry forward to catch her.

My pace slows when we approach the water. I don't want to end up in it. I carefully step to the edge and bend my neck. The water is cool to the touch of my tongue. I take three big gulps.

"Can we walk through the creek?" Ben asks.

"Yeah! Let's do it!" Lucy agrees. "Please, Mom?"

"What about the dogs?" Hannah asks.

"They can come with us," Nate says.

"They don't like the water," Hannah says. Nate shrugs his shoulders. "Okay. Lead the way, Ben. Be careful, some of the rocks may be slippery."

Ben steps forward on a rock, careful to not touch the water. He takes a few more steps to the middle of the water on a path of rocks.

"Come on, Zelda," he says.

There's no way I am going in there. One wrong step and I'm Zelda the soaking wet pug. No way.

I hear a small splash and turn. Peach is in the water, taking one slow step at a time on her way to Ben. The water covers the white on her paws. Nate follows behind with her leash, sidestepping on the rocks.

I can't believe she is in the water!

Peach doesn't like the water and rain, except for the one time we stayed away from home for a week. Peach and I ran in the edge of the moving water every day. That was fun.

Does Peach have the right idea? Maybe I should give this water a try.

Ben looks at me from his spot on the rock a few steps away. The leash won't go any farther. I look to Peach. The water was cold on my tongue, and the squirrels are in the trees. *I think I'll stay out of it for now.* I turn to walk forward in the dirt on the side of the water.

"Mom, can you take Zelda? I don't think she will come in the water," Ben says.

"Sure." The leash sails through the air to Hannah. Lucy follows her dad to the middle of the water. Ben, Lucy, Nate, and Peach wander forward through the water and rocks.

Hannah and I skip along the side of the water. I sniff some trees, looking for squirrel traces, until Hannah yanks me forward. We walk for a few minutes. I keep my head on a swivel, glancing at my family in the middle of the water. Peach hasn't left the water. Her paws are soaked, but her tongue hangs out of her mouth as she trots forward with the rest of the family.

I turn back to my path along the side of the river. I take a step, and my paws sink into warm, moist dirt.

Mud!

My tail bounces on my back, and I step again.

"Zelda, get out of there," Hannah says.

I take another step. All four of my paws are in the patch of warm mud. It feels wonderful.

"Zelda, go," Hannah says. The leash tugs my harness. I turn to Hannah and give her my best sad pug eyes.

"ARRFF!"

My ears perk up at the sound of Peach's bark. She is sprinting in circles through the water. The water trail has transformed into a big open space with mud and rocks in the center. On the side opposite from me, water falls from the side of the tall rock.

I look at Peach with her tongue hanging out and her ears straight in the air. She is having a blast. Ben chases her through the water, splashing water in every direction. Lucy lets out a loud laugh.

They can't have fun without me!

I look at the path to them. The rocks are scattered, but I can make it without getting in the water. I leap to the first rock, and my paws slide, but I dig my nails in and stop. The rest of the rocks are smaller. To make it, I have to make one big series of jumps on the small rocks until the mud patch in the middle. I take a deep breath, sneeze, and let my tongue hang out. If I make this without falling, it will be legendary.

Ready. Set. Go.

I make the first leap and then the next. Before I know it, I have jumped four times. The path to the mud is the best game I have ever played. I bounce from one rock to the next over the water, listening to my family's laughs and shouts of glee. I hop and skip and jump.

I am the jumping pug! Only four more jumps.

I sail in the air and land on a rock. I quickly leap to the next.

This rock is slick. *Uh oh.* I'm sliding. I push off the rock to make the next leap, but something isn't right. My paws flail as I fly through the air, and I hit the water with a big splash.

The splash sends water flying in all directions, but the water doesn't even reach my belly. I shake off the water and look at my family. They smile. I realize that Hannah has let go of my leash.

Peach bounds over to me, and I stand on my hind legs to greet her.

"Zelda, wait," Nate says. I freeze, and Nate unhooks the leash from my harness. Peach is already unhooked. I look at her. Her eyes widen, and I run, forgetting the water. She chases after me, and we run in circles through the water. When I am breathing too hard to continue, I stop and plop in the water. My body sinks into the combination of water and mud.

This is great.

"I think they like the creek," Ben says.

"Come on, let's keep walking," Nate says. Nate and Ben walk out of the water and up a dirt path. Peach is already out of the water, trailing behind them. I scamper to catch up. Lucy and Hannah walk behind me. Nate leads us to the top of the small hill, and when we get there, I see another water trail.

This time, I run straight into the water, not afraid to get wet. Water doesn't scare me anymore. In fact, I don't think anything scares me anymore. I feel invincible. I sprint ahead, leaping from a rock into the water.

Nothing can stop this pug!

We leave the water trail later in the day. My paws are cold, and my legs are exhausted. I jump into the back of the car. When I land, a drop of water trickles from my ear. The feeling sends me into a head shake.

"Zelda! No!" Hannah shouts, but I ignore her scream. My head shake transforms into a full body shake, sending sprinkles of water from my fur in every direction. When I stop, Ben glares at me.

"Dad, the car is soaked," he says.

"It's not a long drive. You will be fine."

"You don't have to sit with a sopping wet pug on you," Ben murmurs.

I move to the middle of the car to allow Ben to sit. Lucy steps in the car on the other side. Peach jumps in on top of her.

"Peach isn't that wet," Lucy says.

"Lucky," Ben says. Ben sets a blanket on his lap, and I curl up in it. The water trapped in my fur sends a chill through me. Ben wraps me up in the blanket, and moments later I am dreaming of squirrels and steak.

I jerk awake when the car comes to a stop. I hear Peach snoring on the other side of the car. I open my eyes and stand to look out the window.

Home.

I'm relieved. I had a blast today, but I am ready to eat a good meal and sleep the rest of the day away.

"Ben, keep Zelda and Peach outside until I get the water ready."

Huh?

I wander around in the front yard until the door opens.

"Okay. Bring them here, but don't take them off their leash."

Peach and I jog to Hannah, excited to get inside. When I cross through the doorway, I freeze. I hear the sound. *Oh no. Not now.* My tail sinks, and I try to hide behind Ben.

"Come on, Zelda. It's okay," Hannah says. Ben hands the leash to his mom and wanders up the stairs. I look to Peach. Her eyes are open wide, and I can tell she has checked into her happy place.

"Nate, can you help me with Peach?"

"Sure, honey." Nate comes around the corner and lifts Peach in the air.

Hannah bends down to scoop me up, and I go limp in her arms. They take us into the small room. The rushing sound is loud, and I hate it. It's not the sound, but what it means. The sound stops. Nate lifts Peach into the giant bowl. Hannah drops me beside her. The water rises to my stomach. I expect a chill to rise through me, but it doesn't. Instead, the water warms my body.

I know what is coming next, and I want to get out of this big bowl. I don't care if the water feels good this time. I hate being trapped. I grunt and think about going for a leap over the edge. I've made the jump before, but it's always risky. I don't want to end up falling under the water. Before I decide what to do, Hannah puts a glob of something on my back and runs her hands over my body. She massages it through my body, giving me a not-pug smell. I don't like it. I never like it. I have to get out of here, but her hands are all over me.

She takes a break for a second, and I ready myself, but before I can move, her hands steady me again. I look at Peach. Peach is staring off into space. She is trapped in a faraway place in her head.

Water pours over me, and Hannah runs her hands through my fur again, steadying me, not letting me move. I close my eyes and wait for the water to stop. When her hands leave my body, I am sopping wet again. I feel the water dropping from all over me.

"Zelda, wait," Hannah says.

I can't wait.

I go for it.

I leap out of the bowl and land on solid ground. I shake my hardest, freeing my fur from all the water on me.

"Zelda," Nate moans, but I shake more. When I stop, I check my surroundings.

The door is closed!

I scurry to the door, but Hannah lifts me into a blanket. The blanket rubs against my fur. I squirm, but she has a firm grip. Finally, she sets me on the ground and opens the door.

I sprint out the door and through the house. I run from room to room shaking off the water and getting as far away from what just happened until I hear the sound of Peach's paws and breath behind me. She catches me, and we tumble on the ground. We wrestle until I topple over, out of breath, the memory of the washing far from my little head.

I head to the living room and find Lucy on the couch. I snuggle up to her, and she covers me up. Today was another exhausting day, but a good day as Zelda pug.

Chapter 2
The Dog Park

The next day, I wait by the front door in expectation of another car ride. When my family leaves during the bright hours without us, I realize we aren't returning to the water trail today.

Gradually, I return to a normal routine and stop waiting by the door. We haven't returned to the water trail. I hope it wasn't a one-time outing, but I have enough adventures awaiting me in my neighborhood to fill my time. I spend the mornings and evenings in the backyard. I think of exploring beyond the fence, but I don't have a good reason to risk it.

The days fade into one another, but when I hear the word "park" one day, my ears perk up.

I scamper to Nate and Ben to listen to their conversation. I don't understand many of the words, but the words "dog" and "park" are enough to make my tail bounce. When I hear Nate say, "Let's go," I know it's time for another adventure. I follow Ben to the front of the house. He takes the harnesses off the shelf.

Yes!

I pug sprint in circles through the room. With the commotion, Peach wanders into the room. I run around her. She nips at me and then grabs a toy. I reach for the toy and grab it with my mouth. As we play tug-of-war, I forget why I am excited.

"Peach, come," Nate says. Peach drops the toy and walks to Nate. I grab the toy and watch Nate put on her harness.

Oh, yeah! Park!

I dart to Ben. He grabs me and places the harness around my body.

The car ride is short. We park in a large grassy area. I jump out of the car, and the smells attack my nose.

So many dogs!

Peach and I, sniffing and tracking, scamper from one smell to the next. Ben and Nate try to keep us moving forward. As we approach a fence, the smells grow more potent. A dog barks. Ben and Nate let us in the fence.

When I enter the fence, I realize that I have been to this park. My family brought us here for my fourth birthday. The park was filled with pugs. I ran with them for an hour. It was amazing. My nose tells me the pugs aren't here today, but that's okay. *I'll run with any dog!*

Hannah and Nate take off our leashes and let us through another gate. I see two small dogs chasing each other through the open grass. Peach takes off for the dogs, catching them in an instant.

Geez. She is fast.

I investigate a few smells along the fence, and I spot another dog on the other side of the fence. The dog reminds me of Norman with its gigantic head and wrinkles. Norman and I love playing, even though he is much bigger than me. I bark at the dog, trying to get its attention. The dog races to the fence and barks at me. The bark is playful, so I take off running next to the fence. He races with me on the other side of the fence. We run back and forth for a few minutes, but then another dog enters his side. He takes off running with it. I stop.

Peach stands near Ben and Nate. I jog to them. A water bowl rests next to Ben, so I take a drink. When the Norman look-alike barks, I jog back to the fence with Peach beside me. The other side of the fence is filled with dogs. The dogs are bigger than we are, but they are running and playing all over the grass.

Peach notices all the dogs and leaps straight up in the air. Her head reaches the top of the fence. She wants to go to the other side of the fence too. I paw at the fence and bark. A pug-colored dog comes to the fence on the other side. He tries to lick my face through the fence.

"Peach, Zelda," Nate shouts. Peach stops her leaping. We both turn and face Nate. He stands by the gate. I look at Peach. We bark in unison, and then we sprint to him. He opens the gate in the nick of time. Peach and I dash through to the other side. I see the group of big dogs and run straight for them.

Peach beats me to the dogs. A black dog sprints away, so Peach chases after it. I run to the group of dogs and weave in and out of them, baiting one of them to come after me. The dog that tried to lick me through the fence takes the bait. He chases after me. He is fast, but my short pug legs can turn on a dime. I change direction moments before he catches me. Then we are off again. I head for a tree to maneuver away from the dog, but he is too fast.

He catches up to me. I freeze. So does he. We stand with our butts in the air in a standoff.

He has a twinkle in his eyes, and I pounce for him. Even though he is much bigger than me, I can stand my own. We tumble through the grass. I roll back on to my belly and bark, but then Peach comes racing between us with the black dog in tow.

Peach!

I chase after them, and my new friend follows. We run through the entire area, and as we run, more and more dogs join our game of chase. A skinny gray dog joins the fun. She runs with a grace unlike any other dog I have seen. It's almost like she is flying through the air. She catches Peach in an instant, and Peach collapses in the grass. All the dogs chasing Peach stop. We pant, tired and out of breath.

I jog to Ben and Nate. They have the water bowl, and I stop to get my fill. Peach follows me and takes a few long gulps. Then she collapses on the grass on her side, panting with her tongue hanging out.

"I think they like running with the big dogs," Ben says.

"No kidding," Nate replies.

"I can't believe Zelda can keep up with them."

What? Of course I can keep up with them.

Ben's words light a fire inside of me. I might not be as big or as fast as some of the other dogs, but I make up for my lack of speed and size with my pug smarts and stubbornness. I look to the skinny gray dog running around the exterior of the park. If I catch him, everyone will know that I am the top dog.

I go for a jog through the park to scope out the area. An idea pops into my pug brain. I take off for the gray dog. We cross paths in the middle of the field, but he doesn't pause for me. He darts forward with a few dogs behind him.

Well. That didn't work.

I watch him run and recognize the pattern of his gallop through the park. I join in the chase, knowing I can't catch him a dead sprint. When we reach a tree, I stop. Ben and Nate are sitting on a bench a few steps away.

Perfect.

I hide behind the trunk and wait, listening to the noises of the paws trampling through the park. The gray dog is very soft on his paws, barely making a sound, but I know he is coming.

I jump out from behind the tree. The gray dog lets out a yelp and then scatters in the other direction. Ben and Nate laugh. I plop on the ground and let my tongue hang out.

"Did you see that?" Ben asks. Nate nods. "Zelda scared that greyhound."

"I know," Nate says.

"Zelda is crazy."

"No, she's not crazy. She's smart."

True.

"Yep. We should make a cartoon series. We can call it 'The Legend of Zelda'," Ben says. Nate laughs.

Ben called me a legend!

"I don't think we can call it that. Copyright mumbo jumbo."

"Right."

"ARRFF! ARRFF!"

Peach barrels toward me with a dog on her tail. I sidestep out of the way as they race past.

"Zelda, Peach, time to go," shouts Nate.

I stand and walk to them. My tail bounces from one side of my butt to the other. Peach hurries to my side. As we walk out of the dog park together, I don't acknowledge or bark at the other dogs, but I walk with a strut to my step. All the dogs know the truth. I am the pug legend.

Chapter 3
The House Sitters

After a few uneventful days, my family begins to act in a strange manner. Hannah and Nate stuff a bag full of clothes and take it to the front door. Ben brings another bag to the door. They are packing for a trip!

I dash to the living room. My toys haven't moved. Neither has my food. Maybe my family hasn't packed up my stuff yet? I can't imagine they would go on a trip without Peach and me.

I sit on my perch on the couch, staring outside and waiting for my chance to run out the door with my family. My family eats dinner and settles into a typical evening together. The bags rest by the front door.

The next morning, Nate and Ben load the car with the bags. I wait by the door until I hear a knock on the door. I bark until Nate opens the door. A familiar face from the neighborhood enters the house. She has a bag in her hand.

"Hi, Becky," Hannah says. Peach runs to her and licks her hand. I stay back, wary of the stranger.

"Hi, Peach," Becky says.

"Peach, off," Hannah says. "You'll have plenty of time to give Becky kisses over the next week."

The next week? What?

"Come on, let me show you around the house."

I follow Hannah and Becky up the steps.

"This is our guest room and your room for the week." They walk to the bathroom and then back down the stairs.

"What do I need to know about Zelda and Peach?"

"The food is in the cupboard. Give them half a bowl in the morning and evening. Besides that, they tell you when they want to go out by waiting by the back door. Zelda even tells you if she wants to go for a walk. She will sit by the front door."

Becky chuckles. "Really?" Hannah nods. "Should I walk them everyday?" Becky asks.

"If you can, that would be great. They love walks." *Yes, we do.*

"Anything else?"

"Not really. They are pretty good dogs." *Pretty good? How about amazing?*

"Ready to go?" Nate asks as he walks into the kitchen. Hannah looks to Becky.

"I'm set," she says.

"Perfect. Thanks so much, Becky," Nate says. "We don't like to kennel them for a week, so this is a big help for us."

"Call if you need anything," Hannah says. "The vet number is on the fridge, but you shouldn't need that."

"I hope not," she says.

"Ben, Lucy, say good-bye to Zelda and Peach."

Lucy runs over to me. She picks me up and squeezes me. I put on my tough pug act and sneeze, but I will miss her. I can't remember the length of a week, but it sounds too long for my family to be away.

She sets me on the floor. Ben pets my head. Peach gives long kisses to Ben and Lucy. Then my family says one more good-bye and walks out the door.

Through the window from my perch on the couch, I watch the car pull away. I sigh, but it turns into a sneeze. Peach wanders over to me. She paws at me, so I jump on the couch. I don't feel like playing, but I realize that Peach doesn't either. She curls up next to me, and we fall asleep, hoping our family returns soon.

I awake to thumps and bangs coming from the kitchen. I leap off the couch and dash toward the action. Becky stands in the kitchen, opening and closing all the cupboard doors and drawers. I run to her and bark to get her to stop making so much noise. She stops and looks at me.

"Hi, Zelda," she says. "Do you know where they keep your treats?" *Treats?* She opens another cupboard. "I forgot to ask, and I don't see them in the closet with your food." *Yep. Because I can get to them there.*

I stroll across the kitchen and stare at the cupboard above the sink. Becky meanders on the other side of the kitchen, opening and closing more doors by the dog food. I bark again. She spins around. I bark and stare above the sink. *When is she going to get the hint?*

"What Zelda?" she asks. I stare at the cabinet. After I stare for too long, she walks to me and looks at the cabinet above the sink. She opens it and then stares back at me wide-eyed.

"You knew the treats were in here. You were trying to tell me."

Yes. Duh.

"You are a smart pug." She grabs the bag of peanut butter goobers, crinkling the bag. The noise causes Peach to race into the kitchen. She body-slams me out of the way and jumps sky high for the treats.

"Woah," Becky says. "Sit." We both sit in front of her. She hands each of us a full-size goober treat. I scarf it before she realizes her mistake. I want another. I sit in front of her waiting. I lick my nose in anticipation. Peach jumps in the air in front of me.

"Okay. I'll give you another." She bends down and hands us each another full-size treat.

Awesome! I never get full-size goobers!

Becky places the bag of treats back in the cabinet and walks into the living room. I settle into my spot in the couch, and Peach joins me. We fall asleep.

When we wake up, the light is beginning to fade outside. Peach and I go outside in the back until the darkness overwhelms us. Tired, I plop on the couch on the fuzzy blanket. Peach wanders upstairs. A few minutes later, she comes back downstairs. Her eyes are bugging out more than normal. She doesn't know what to do. Usually she sleeps in bed with Lucy and me, or with Hannah and Nate if the kids are gone. But now everyone is gone. I look at her and turn my head. She leaps on the couch and cuddles with me. I don't normally cuddle with Peach, but I can tell she is upset. This is the first time the family is away from her. I'll have to keep her happy for the next week.

The next day, I strategize how to get more treats from Becky. Somehow I have to convince Becky that I am worthy of treats all the time. I need to impress her.

The first part of my plan is to showcase my walking skills. Honestly, my walking skills aren't great. I get distracted too easily, but for a treat and to impress Becky, I will be the best walking dog on the street.

I wait by the front door so Becky knows it's walking time. After a few minutes, she notices me.

"Okay. We can go for a walk."

Perfect.

I run in circles around her, completing my normal pre-walk dance.

"Zelda, stay," Becky shouts, but I don't listen. I skip away from her reach. She sighs and picks up Peach's harness.

"Peach, do you want to go for a walk?"

Peach groans, stretches, and jumps down from the couch. She walks to Becky and doesn't struggle one bit when Becky slips the harness over her body.

"Good girl," Becky says. She turns to me. "Okay, Zelda. Your turn."

I stare at her, debating my next move. If I behave, that will impress her and turn her in my favor for the treats. I should cooperate.

She takes a step in my direction. I wait. She takes one more step and reaches down with the harness in her hand.

I can't resist.

I dart out from under her hands in the other direction. She chases after me. We run in circles through the living room. My tail bounces from one side to the next. I pause for a second, and she lunges. This time I freeze, and she places the harness around me.

"Finally," she murmurs. Becky leashes me and opens the front door. Peach and I burst forward down the steps. We lead her through the neighborhood, stopping at our favorite trees and light posts. I don't bark at any dogs!

When we return to the house, she leads us inside. I go to the kitchen and sit on the floor under the treat cabinet, but she never comes. *I guess I need a new plan.*

I return to the living room. Peach is cuddled with Becky on the couch. I lie in the dog bed and brainstorm new ideas, but my eyes close, and I fall asleep.

When I awaken, I have the perfect idea. I glance around the room. My nap must have been short. Peach and Becky are still on the couch. I don't see anything in the room that will work for my plan, so I run upstairs to Lucy's room. I jump on the bed and grab the fuzzy blanket. I drag the blanket down the steps, careful not to trip or stumble. When the blanket and I arrive downstairs in the living room, I pull the blanket to the middle of the floor. Becky gives me a weird look but does nothing, so I run up the stairs again.

Ben's room is a mess, but I don't see anything I can grab with my mouth. I walk to the other side of the bed into the half-open closet door. *Jackpot.* I bite a little man and take him downstairs. I drop him on the blanket and run back up the stairs without looking at Becky. I hear footsteps behind me, but I scurry into Becky's room-for-the-week. Her open bag rests on the floor. I push through the bag with my nose and find a few socks. I grab two and turn around.

Becky is staring at me. I dash between her legs and scamper down the stairs. I lie on Lucy's blanket and start chewing on the sock, waiting for Becky. I can hear her feet on the stairs. Peach opens her eyes and looks at me.

"Zelda," Becky says. "Give me that." She takes a few steps closer, attempting to trap me. I dart across the room with her sock in my mouth.

"Zelda, drop it." I ignore her and sprint across the room to the opening behind the couch.

"Zelda, come." I sit and wait. She tries a few more times to get me out from behind the couch, but she can't reach me. She stomps away, and I hear the squeak of cabinet opening in the kitchen.

Yes!

With the crinkle of the treat bag, I hear the thump of Peach landing on the floor and then the click of her nails hitting the floor as she runs to the kitchen. The clicks stop. Peach must be eating a treat. Then the clinks come toward me. Becky appears at the end of the couch.

"Want a treat, Zelda?"

Yes!

"Come, here." She places a treat on the floor right in front of the couch. I drop the sock, grab the treat, and back up before she can grab me. She groans.

"Zelda."

She's going to hate me, but it's only for a week. Treats are worth it. I can tell she is trying to outsmart me. That is not going to happen. I am the smartest pug around. I am the queen of this house.

Becky keeps the treat in her hand, but she calls for me. I don't move. After a few minutes of the standoff, she does exactly what I thought she would. *Amateur.* She places a trail of treats from the start of the couch to the middle of the floor. Her plan is to grab me or the sock when I follow the treat trail. She doesn't know that I just did this for the treats.

I take the bait and run for the treats, gobbling all seven of them. I expect Becky to snatch me at any moment, but she doesn't! She takes her sock and goes upstairs. *Even better!* I'm so happy that I leave two treats for Peach. This is the stuff of pug dreams!

Becky comes back downstairs. I jump on the couch next to her and lie so I'm touching her legs. I'm trying to get back in her good graces.

She pets my head, and I know I'll be okay for the rest of the time my family is away.

Over the next few days, I sucker Becky into giving us a few more treats. I even force her to take me on four walks in one day. *Four!* Yet even with the four-walk day and the many treats, I can't wait for my family to come home.

I know they are coming soon because Becky put all her stuff in her bag and cleaned up the house. I wait on the couch looking out the window. When I see the car pull into the driveway, I jump off the couch and bark at Peach. She checks the window, and we scratch at the front door.

My family bursts through the door, and my adrenaline takes over. I sprint from Ben to Lucy to Nate to Hannah and back to Lucy. I lick everyone's hands and even a few faces when they bend over. Soon the licks turn into sneezes, but my family doesn't mind. They are happy to see me.

When I manage to get my tail to stop bouncing, I sit in Lucy's lap on the couch. I listen to Hannah and Nate ask a few questions of Becky. Becky doesn't say a word about the sock incident. In fact, she says the week went great.

I can get away with anything these days.

After Becky leaves, my family carries a bunch of bags in the house. They empty the bags and settle in the living room. I bring an owl to Nate, and we play keep-away. Ben tosses tennis balls to Peach.

After an hour of playing, we go upstairs. Peach and I cuddle with Lucy and close our eyes. Soon I hear the sleep-breathing of Lucy and the snoring of Peach. I close my eyes. Everything is right. Everything is perfect.

Chapter 4
The Cone of Shame

I wake up to the darkness of the middle of the night. I am under the blankets. It's too hot. I slither my way forward to get fresh air, but I can't get out. Peach must be lying on top of the blankets. I turn around and step over Lucy under the blankets. There isn't much space before the bed ends on this side, but I creep forward and poke my head out on the pillow. The fresh air feels great. I close my eyes.

Something jerks me out of sleep later that night. My tongue is dry, so I need water. I can't see, but I jump to the floor to find water. I step forward. The water bowl should be in front of me, but I can't find it. Frustrated, I turn around quickly and smash forehead first into the corner of the bed.

Pain surges through one of my eyes. I crumple to the floor. My body trembles. I blink several times, hoping the blinking will flush out what is hurting my eye. It doesn't help. Maybe I can get it out with my paw. I paw at my eye, but the pain only worsens the longer my eye is open. It feels terrible.

I don't know what to do.

I lie shaking on the floor, eyes closed. Maybe I can sleep it off. I try to relax, but I can't settle down. In a panic, I hurry into Hannah and Nate's room. I can't jump on the bed because I can't see, so I lie on the ground next to their bed, whimpering and groaning.

Please wake up.

The pain is terrible. I think I'm going to lose my eye. *Oh no. Hannah. Nate. Please.*

I hear a stirring on the bed.

"What is that?" Hannah mumbles. She flips on a light and shines it my direction. With my one open eye, I see her glance at me on the floor.

"Zelda, what's going on?" She picks me up and sets me on the bed. I shake and paw at my eye. "It's okay," she says, petting my head.

"Nate, wake up."

He grumbles something and eventually rolls over. "What?"

"Zelda. Something is wrong with her."

I hear and feel Nate move on the bed, but both of my eyes are closed now. I'm trying to relax, hoping my eye will be okay.

"I think it's her eye."

I feel Nate's hands around me. He moves me into his lap. I open my one eye and look at him. The lights are on now.

"Hi, Zelda. Can you open the other eye?" He reaches toward my face, but I squirm. He gets a firm grip, and I feel his fingers on my eye. I let out a squeal as he lifts my eyelids. I squirm and fidget, and his fingers move away from my eye.

"She's definitely in pain. Something is wrong with the eye. What time is it?" he asks.

"Two in the morning."

"Let's give her fifteen minutes to see if she will calm down and sleep. If not, we need to take her to the emergency vet."

Vet? I don't want to go there. Is Gannondorf back?

The shaking worsens. I can't stop it.

"Okay. I'll look up the closest place to take her."

I hear Hannah move out of the room. Nate continues to pet my head. It feels good to be in his arms, but I can't shake the panic and the pain I feel. The shaking continues. My heart races in my chest, and I want to run, to get away from all this, to feel better. I force my body into motion, but Nate reigns me in before I go anywhere.

"Zelda, it's okay," he says.

But I don't believe him.

"The closest vet is about twenty minutes away. I called to double-check that they are open."

"We should take her. She isn't settling down, and her heart is beating too fast for her little pug body. Plus, she keeps trying to run away from me."

"Wake the kids?" Hannah asks.

"I think so. One of us will have to hold her while the other drives."

"I'll hurry."

I listen to the sounds of Ben and Lucy moving. Nate hands me to Hannah, and she carries me down the stairs. Soon we are in the car driving somewhere. I can't remember where they said we were going now. The pain is too great. I can't focus.

When we stop, Nate carries me inside. I peek my good eye open, but it is dark outside. I don't recognize anything. Inside, the place reeks of dogs, but I can't concentrate to make out the smells. I hear Hannah and Nate talking. I am handed to someone new, but I don't fight it anymore. I shake uncontrollably as fingers grapple me. They try to open my eye, but I can't let them. It's too painful. They stop poking. I feel a quick stab of pain in my side and then everything goes black.

When I wake up, a lady is passing me into Nate's arms. I feel so tired, but my eye feels okay. I lift my head up, but something stops me. I have something around my head.

What is this?

I try to figure it out, but my fatigue overtakes me. They carry me to the car, and I pass out.

When I open my eyes, I am in my dog bed, but the bed is on the floor of Hannah and Nate's room. My eye aches, but it doesn't hurt like last night. Something is tied around my head. I stand and realize it's like a shield that comes out past my face. It's heavy around my small head. I walk, but when I look down, the shield trips me. *Ugh.*

"Come on Zelda. Let me help you." Hannah scoops me into her arms and carries me down the stairs. She places me on the couch next to Nate. He is sipping coffee.

"Hi, Zelda." He pets my back. "Your eye isn't green anymore. That's a good sign."

I sit in his lap, hoping he will take off the shield. He doesn't. I lie for a few minutes before I stand. I need some water. I walk to the edge of the couch. Before I can jump, Nate lifts me to the ground.

"That's not a good idea right now," he says.

What? I can't jump anymore? I wander into the kitchen, taking it slow so I don't hit anything with my head shield. I go to the water bowl, but I can't reach the water with this stupid thing. This cone might be worse than Gannondorf, the tapeworm.

"Here, Zelda." Hannah puts a large bowl on the other side of the kitchen. I take gulp after gulp. The water feels great in my dry mouth. When I finish, I go to the back door and sit.

"Nate, Zelda wants to go out."

"Okay." Nate puts on shoes and picks me up. He sets me on the grass in the back. The sunshine stings my eye. Plus walking and getting around with this thing on my head is not easy. A few days ago, I was the queen of this house and a legend in the dog park. Now I can't even walk straight.

What happened?

I sulk through the yard back to the door. Peach is waiting by the door. Nate lifts me up the steps into the house. He lets Peach out. She runs free through the backyard. I watch from inside the door, wondering if that will ever be me again.

The day passes by slowly. I am stuck spending most of the day on the couch. I can't do much because of my cone head. I think that's what Hannah and Nate called it. Lucy has stayed by my side most of the day, petting me and keeping me company, but I miss my adventures and mischief. Peach keeps checking on me and trying to lick my face, but she can't reach it because of the cone.

My eye hurts from time to time. When it hurts, I close my eyes and sleep it off. Usually when I wake up, it feels better for a bit, so I get some water or food. Then I lie down again, and the cycle repeats.

When the darkness comes, Hannah and Nate take me into their room. I sit on the dog bed, looking at their bed.

"Okay, Zelda," Hannah says. She lifts me on the bed. I try to cuddle with her, but the cone gets in the way. Frustrated, I groan and plop down. "Do you think we can take the cone off for the night?" My ears perk up.

"I don't know. What if she scratches her eye in the middle of the night?"

"Yeah. I guess you are right. Let's keep it on."

"At least for tonight. Maybe tomorrow we can see how she reacts to it being off." Hannah nods, and a small gleam of hope fills me. Maybe the cone won't be on my head forever.

The next morning Hannah takes the cone off my head. The freedom of head movement is wonderful. I can eat and drink without having to concentrate on lining up the cone with the bowl.

They let me outside into the bright sunshine. I run through the backyard, but after a couple minutes, my eye is burning again.

Oh no.

I run to the back door and lie on the couch with my eyes closed. The burning fades after a long time. I move around the house again, but I have to take it easy now. I can't be the pug legend anymore. I have to be a boring, run-of-the-mill pug. I sigh and plop in Lucy's lap, hoping one day I will be the adventurous pug again.

Chapter 5

The Race

Even with the cone off my head, I take it easy by spending most of the day indoors on the couch. My angry bird taunts me, but I don't play with it. After four dark sleeps, I step outside into the bright morning light. For the first time, my eye doesn't burn or even ache, so I take off, sprinting in a circle through the backyard. But after I run one lap, a terrible thought enters my little head. I stop. What if I slip and tumble? What if Peach chases me and swipes my eye by accident? I can't risk another injury. I trot to the door, and Nate lets me inside the house.

I reclaim my spot on the couch and sleep away the next day. I wake up the next morning to almost darkness, but my face is stirring in the house. I head down the stairs to see what they are up to before the morning light is out. Lucy and Ben are eating at the table. Hannah is wearing her walking shoes.

"We need to leave in a few minutes," Hannah says.

"I'm ready," Nate says. Ben stands from the table and takes his bowl to the sink. He runs up the stairs. Hannah takes Lucy's bowl to the sink. Lucy puts on her shoes.

"Zelda, go outside," Nate says. He opens the door, and I oblige. Peach joins me outside a few minutes later.

When we return inside, Nate has our harnesses in his hand. He puts Peach's harness on her first. Without thinking, I start my pre-walk dance through the living room. Nate is quick this morning. He catches me after one circle, and we leave through the back door.

Wait a minute. A car ride?

I bounce from one side of the car to the other. I stand on Lucy's lap and look out the window, but the car turns to the right. I fall forehead first into the glass narrowly missing smashing my eyes into the window.

Ow.

That was a close one. I shake it off and back away from the window. I settle into Lucy's lap.

We arrive a few minutes later. People and cars are everywhere. Hannah and Peach lead the way through the crowd. I stay close to Ben's side, afraid to get trampled. Nate leads us to a calm spot in the grass. After sneezing seven times, I investigate the grass with Peach while we wait for Hannah. She has disappeared in the crowd of people.

A smell invades my nose. Another dog is near. I look up, but I can't see anything through the crowd of people. I look to Peach. Her ears are standing straight in the air, facing forward. She is on high alert. I pull my leash in the direction of the smell, but Ben yanks me the other way. The yank causes a wisp of pain to flutter through my head.

Oh no. I can't pull on the leash. That's a bummer.

I sit in the grass and wait. I watch Hannah walk through the crowd to us.

"Ready to run?" she asks Peach.

Wait, what?

She takes Peach's leash.

"We will cheer you two on from the course," Nate says.

"Good luck Mom," Lucy says.

"Beat all the other dogs," Ben says.

What is Peach doing? Why am I not going?"

Hannah smiles, waves, and then leads Peach away from us. They disappear into the crowd.

Hannah took Peach with her? What is going on?

I slink further into the grass and lie down.

"Let's find a place to watch the race," Nate says. He leads us through the people. I sidestep through all the feet and legs, trying to avoid an accidental stomp on my little pug body. We stop at a place in the grass close to the road. A loud boom echoes, and my fur stands in the air on my back.

"Daddy, what was that?"

"It's okay, Lucy. That's the start of the race."

"Do you think that Peach will run the whole time?" Ben asks.

"I don't know."

"I think she will," Lucy says. From down the small street, I see a group of people approaching at a fast clip. They scurry past, but I see no sign of Peach or Hannah.

"Where is Mom?" Lucy asks again.

"She's coming," Nate says.

I sit and wait, staring at the street. I catch a faint trace of Peach in the air before I see her. Peach and Hannah are jogging on the path together. Peach's eyes are wide open, as usual. She is running beside Hannah.

"Good job, Honey," Nate shouts. She smiles and waves.

"Go, Peach, go!" Ben yells. Peach doesn't turn her attention from the road in front of her. She keeps running and in an instant they turn the corner and vanish from sight. A moment later, a man and his big brown dog jog past.

Peach isn't the only dog running!

My first instinct is to chase the dog, but I stop myself. I can't pull on the leash. But I also don't want to be stuck on the sidelines.

"Time to move to the next spot. It's close to the finish." Nate leads us across another grassy field. I can't believe that Peach is on a run or walk or whatever it is without me.

We stop close to the small road again and wait. The people on the path approach one at a time.

"There they are," Ben says. He points across the way to the path winding around the corner. I see Hannah and Peach. They are running together. As they approach, I see Peach's tongue bouncing outside her mouth. She is having so much fun.

"Finish strong!" Nate shouts.

"Good job, Peach," Lucy says. Ben whistles. Hannah waves as they run past us on the path.

"Come on," Nate says. He jogs forward following the side of the path. People line each side shouting and clapping. We hurry into the cluster of people. I see Hannah and Peach ahead. Hannah is bent over, breathing hard. Peach has plopped on the grass with her tongue hanging out.

"Great job," Nate says.

"Peach was the first dog to finish!" Lucy says.

"She did great," Hannah says, in between breaths. Nate grabs a bowl from a bag. He places it in front of Peach and empties water into the bowl. Peach drinks the water in seconds, and he refills it. I walk to Hannah and give her a lick on the hand.

"Thanks, Zelda," she says. "Ready to go?"

"Only if you are," Nate says. "We can hang out here for a bit if you want."

"Let's go. I could use a shower." Nate and Hannah lead us across the grass in a slow walk. I trail behind them with my tail limp. A week ago, I was the one in the spotlight. I love Peach, but I should be running with Hannah, too. Somehow I have to figure out how to move forward, past the pain and the fear of getting hurt. I have to regain my bold pug spirit. But how?

Chapter 6
The Rain Storm

During the next few days, I start to take a few risks in hopes I can move forward. I play with Lucy and run around in the backyard. Peach instigates a game of chase with me. We sprint through the backyard. The playing helps me feel more normal, but I know I'm not one hundred percent. When Peach tries to wrestle, I hide under the bed or behind the couch. I can't get past the fear that a rogue claw will scratch my eye. I need something special to get me out of this rut and to get my confidence back. I look for anything out of the ordinary, like a good old-fashioned adventure or mystery to solve.

This morning, gray pillows fill the sky, covering much of the light. Today is not a day to play outside, so we hurry outside and run back indoors.

The rain begins to fall a little later in the day. The pitter patter of the rain on the roof lulls me to sleep. I drift in and out of consciousness for the entire day, awaking only to scarf some food.

When I awake the next day, the light isn't bright yet. I wander down the stairs. Nate lets me outside. The backyard is wet, and a cool mist soaks my pug fur. I scamper to my spot, then sprint back inside.

Moments later, a loud crack echoes from outside. I hear the whoosh of the wind, followed by the pounding of the rain hitting the ground and the house. A flash of light streams from the window and lights up the sky.

I stalk through the house, figuring out what to do with myself during another rainy day. I am stuck inside again, away from any potential adventures. I don't want to sleep another day away.

I find Peach trembling under the kitchen table. She hates storms. I try to get her out from the table. I bring her an owl, then a tennis ball, and finally a nylabone. She takes all the toys from me, but doesn't budge from her safe spot under the table. I even sneeze in her face, but she doesn't move.

Disappointed, I head to my perch on top of the sofa and watch the storm. The rain falls in streams on the grass, reminding me of the water trail and water walking adventure. That was so much fun. An idea pops into my pug brain. I leap off the couch and run to the back door. I look out at the backyard. It looks wet, but it's not close to a water trail yet.

I go to the living room and find a blanket folded up in the corner of the room. I drag it to the spot in front of the back door. I spread it out and make myself comfortable. I face the backyard. My eyes watch the rain fall as I wait for the backyard to fill up with water.

When my eyes open later in the day to the steady sound of rain. I look in the backyard. Small puddles have formed throughout the yard. *It's still not like the water trail, but it will have to do.*

I stand and bark at the door. Peach comes to my side.

"Nate, can you let them out?" Hannah says.

"Yep. I'm on it." I hear the rumble of footsteps approaching. "Do we have a towel down here?"

"No. Do you need one?"

"I don't need one, but I think the dogs will. It's pretty wet and muddy out there."

"Okay. I'll grab one." Nate slides open the door. I run out into the warm, humid air. The rain is falling in a steady pace. Within minutes, my pug fur has soaked up a ton of water. I run to the back of the yard, splashing with every pug step.

I wait for Peach to catch up, but after a couple minutes, she isn't anywhere near me. I spin my head and see her at the door. She hasn't moved since she came outside. I sprint back to the door. I bark, encouraging her to come with me. She doesn't move.

"Peach, go," Nate urges. After a staring at Peach for a few minutes, Nate walks away from the door and returns with shoes on his feet. He lifts Peach into the air and sets her down further into the backyard.

"Go!" he says again. She turns to go inside. He lifts her again and brings her even further into the backyard. Again, she runs back for the door. On the third try, she gets the hints and wanders through the rain.

I dash to her, trying to get her excited and ready to run with me. But when I run to her, she runs straight for the door. Nate lets her inside, and I am alone.

Peach might not want to stomp through the water, but I do! I dash from one end of the yard to the other, jumping and stomping in as many puddles as possible. After three laps, my body weighs twice as much as normal, but I start another round.

I sprint and leap into the biggest puddle in the yard. The water splashes in every direction, including in my face. The water burns both my eyes for a second. I freeze and resist the urge to paw at my eyes. Instead, I blink a gazillion times. The burning sensation goes away. I look around the yard. The scene is crystal clear.

I'm okay!

The realization sends me on another sprint through the yard. I create a tornado of splashing water in my wake. I run four laps around the yard at frantic pug pace.

"Zelda, inside!" Nate shouts. I stop and look at Nate in the door. "Inside," he says again.

Bummer.

I scamper to the door, sopping wet. Nate scoops me up into his towel and closes the door.

"Hannah, can you get some bath water started?"

"Sure."

"Zelda was having a little too much fun in our backyard swamp," Nate says. I hear a few laughs as Nate smashes the towel all over my body. He carries me through the living room and up the stairs. At the top of the stairs, I hear the worst sound in the world. Maybe it isn't the worst sound–that would be Vacuum, but it's the second worst sound. It's bath time.

Oh no. I didn't think about this part.

I squirm, trying to escape, but he won't let me go. He carries me into the room and dumps me in the giant bowl of water. With Nate's firm grip, I am stuck in here until it's over. At least I had a mini-adventure today. Even with the bath, I feel like I am one paw closer to being the one and only Zelda pug again.

Chapter 7
The Tall Bowls

The light peeks in through the window. Morning is here. I rush down the stairs and peer out the window. The gray is gone! I stand and scratch the back door. Hannah lets me outside into the bright morning light.

When I step outside, I inhale the damp, warm air. My paws sink with each step on the mushy ground. I am tempted to gallop through the yard, but the thought of another bath stops me from sprinting.

A few minutes later, Peach joins me outside. She high-steps through the wet and muddy ground, trying to avoid staining her white paws. She isn't outside for long. I follow her back into the house.

The family is away for the majority of the day, so Peach and I nap while we await their return. Between naps, I decide today is the day that I take my family for a walk. I haven't gone on a walk since the cone.

When they come home, the bright light is fading. I sit by the front door, eager for a walk before the darkness invades. My family ignores me, so I paw at the door and let out a slight whimper.

"Okay, okay. I hear you," Nate says. He jogs up the stairs and returns a few minutes later.

"I'm taking the dogs for a walk," he calls out. "Be back soon."

Hannah nods. Lucy lies, with her eyes closed, snuggled next to Hannah. Ben is out of sight. Nate jingles the leashes, so Peach struts to the front door. He dresses us for our walk, and we scurry out the door.

Nate leads us on our normal loop through the neighborhood. Peach and I stop at the normal spots, like the light post, a few trees, and mailboxes. When we round the corner to make the final turn toward our home, the bright light in the sky is close to the ground. I freeze and stare at the colors surrounding the bright ball. I'm so engrossed in the sight that I don't hear Nate's words.

"Zelda, let's go. Zelda," he says. I snap out of the trance and shake my head three times. The head shake causes me to sneeze twice. I take a step forward, but all I see are black spots. *Oh no. What now?*

"Zelda, walk!" I jerk forward. I need to walk with Nate. I take a few steps and focus on the walking. In between the black spots, I see the sidewalk. While I try to walk straight, I blink a pug million times. The black spots disappear one by one, and I regain my vision. I breathe a sigh of relief and vow never to stare at the bright ball again.

When our house is within sight, I dash to the front door. Lucy is sitting upright next to Hannah. Ben is on the couch. I take a spot next to Lucy on the couch. Peach runs in the house and grabs a ball. Ben slides onto the floor and grabs a bunch of tennis balls. He launches them one at a time, and Peach chases after each one. She doesn't bring any of them back to him. I don't blame her. He is just going to throw another one.

After round one, Ben stands and gathers the tennis balls from all over the room. He sets them in a pile and sits on the floor. He grabs his tall bowl from the table and places it on the ground next to him. I move to the other end of the couch to get a better vantage point on the action.

When I reach the edge of the couch, I smell something. I look down to Ben's tall bowl.

What is in that?

I jump to the floor. Ben is busy playing with Peach. I creep up to the bowl, tail down, in stealth-pug mode. Ben's eyes are focused forward on Peach and away from his bowl next to him. I am out of Hannah's line of sight, too.

I sniff the bowl. I don't recognize the smell, but the bowl is filled with white water. I stick my head close to the bowl and take a quick lick.

The taste is familiar, but I can't place it from my memory. I look up. Ben is busy with Peach. I take a few more licks. The more I drink from the bowl, the more I like it.

I hear a rustling noise beside me. Ben is standing. I hurry away from the bowl and walk to Peach. Ben reaches beside him and lifts the bowl. He drinks the rest of it. Then he takes the bowl away to the kitchen.

I leap on the couch and look around the living room. Another tall bowl rests on the table in front of the couch. There are always tall bowls around. *How come I haven't tried any of them before?* I think about all the deliciousness waiting for me, and I know that this is my next adventure.

The bowls are my new mission. I scope out the different types of tall bowls and where my family places them. Most of the time, they set the bowls on the table in front of the couch, making it difficult—but not impossible—for me to reach. But every once in a while, one is placed on the floor. The floor placement is a jackpot for me. I am three for three on samples of them. Besides Ben's white drink, I sample a tall bowl with super cold water that tastes great and one dark-colored drink. I don't like that one at all, so I'm going to avoid it next time.

After those first three, I hit a standstill in my drink mission. My family doesn't leave any bowls on the floor for many days, so I need to devise a plan to drink from the bowls on the table. The plan is tricky, but I know I can do it.

I go through the activities motions of the day with my heart beating faster than normal. My back fur keeps standing up from excitement, so I hide under the blankets, waiting for the light to fade and the family to gather in the living room.

Hannah and Lucy settle into the living room first, but they don't bring any bowls. I wait on the couch until Nate arrives with a tall bowl. He puts it on the edge of the table in front of the couch.

I step over Lucy and stand next to Nate on the couch. I sniff, trying to get a whiff of the bowl, before I make a move. The smell is faint, but different, new to my pug nostrils.

I have to get a taste.

"Zelda, leave it," Nate says. I look at him and realize I am very close to the bowl. I take a couple steps away. I need Nate's attention elsewhere to sample his drink.

Peach lies on the floor chewing a nylabone. I jump off the couch, use my pug stealth, and sneak up behind her and take the nylabone. She chases after me. We dash through the living room in a big circle. After a couple minutes, I let her grab the nylabone from me. She takes it, but she no longer has an interest in chewing. Peach wants to play. I jump on the couch away from her.

"ARFFF! ARFFF!" Peach barks. She stares at Nate and barks again.

"Okay, I'll play with you," Nate says. He scoots down from the couch.

Perfect. My plan is working.

While he collects the tennis balls, I inch my way closer to the edge of the couch. The table is too far away. I can't get my nose and tongue inside the bowl from the couch. I have to get on the table.

I look at Hannah and Lucy. Their eyes are focused on Nate and the big talking screen. I don't think they are moving from the couch anytime soon. I have to go for it with them present. There's no other option.

I take a deep breath and step over to the coffee table. The table is slick, but I dig in and put both my front paws on the table. My back legs rest on the end of the couch. I lean forward so my mouth is just above the bowl. I take a lick.

The taste is sweet, and I know I want more. I take another lick. I don't hesitate. After the fourth taste, I know my time is running out. I take one more lick, leaning forward so I can reach more of the drink. But when I lean, my not-so-firm footing on the table causes me to slip. I start to slide.

Uh oh. I'm in trouble.

I scramble to regain my balance, my front paws a flurry of movement, but I forget about the tall bowl. One of my paws knocks the bowl, and I watch in horror as it tumbles over onto the table.

I'm sliding, in danger of falling to the floor between the gap of the couch and the table. I push off the table and manage to vault backward onto the couch while I hear lots of shouting.

"What happened?" Nate asks.

"Zelda," Hannah says. "She knocked over your cup."

"How?"

"I don't know. She was on the table."

"Why was she on the coffee table?"

"I don't know."

I leap from the couch and scurry under my blanket in my dog bed. I can't believe I got caught. I was so close. I don't know if I will ever be the pug I was before the cone.

While Nate and Hannah clean up the table, Peach wanders over to me. She licks my face and lies beside me. I snuggle up next to her and fall asleep, dreaming of my former days of glory.

Chapter 8
The Rabbit

I wake up the next day with Peach's head snuggled in my fur. The light streams through the window, brightening the room. I yawn and sneeze twice before I rise from the bed. Peach groans when I move out from under her big head, but then she falls back asleep. I jump to the floor and head down the stairs.

Hannah and Nate are talking in the kitchen. I sit by the door, and they let me outside. I step into the sunlight and listen to the birds talking. I circle the backyard, checking the usual spots for traces of squirrels. I keep my nose on high alert after finding a couple spots with new scents.

I find a place in the middle of the sun and lie in the grass. A soft breeze ruffles through my fur. This day is perfect. I think about the past few weeks and everything that has happened. It's been rough, but I decide that today is the day everything changes. I am ready for adventures. I am ready for anything.

The back door slides open. Peach runs into the backyard. She finds her spot and then sprints in my direction. I stand and await her arrival. A split second before she arrives, I dash in the other direction. Peach chases me, and we run in circles through the yard. When she catches me, we wrestle and tumble through the grass. When we stop rolling, we both stand, panting and smiling. Peach is ready for me to be back to my normal pug-self too.

"Zelda, Peach, inside!" Hannah shouts. We race to the door. Peach inches past me and soars into the house with a flying leap. She slides across the slippery floor and crashes into a chair. I go the other way and take a few long licks at the water bowl. Peach is on the couch now. I join her for our morning nap.

When I wake up, it is time to seek out an adventure, but I need my family's help. They aren't in the living room. I hear creaks from above, so I skip up the stairs. Lucy is playing in her room. Hannah is sitting on a chair. Ben and Nate are nowhere to be found. Hannah is the best option. I walk up to her and bark twice. She looks down at me. I bark again.

"What, Zelda?" she asks. I bark and then run out of the room and down the stairs. I scratch at the front door, but Hannah doesn't follow. I bark again from downstairs and scratch again. I repeat this process a few times before she appears at the top of the steps.

"Okay, Zelda. I get it." She disappears again. I wait. A few minutes later, Hannah and Lucy come down the stairs. Hannah grabs the harness. Peach jumps down from the couch and waits with me at the door. A few minutes later, we step outside to start our walk.

I lead the way, urging Hannah to walk faster, but only until I catch a whiff of a scent in the grass. I stop and investigate. When I determine there is no mystery or adventure linked to the scent, I continue forward. Peach walks at her own pace, stopping for her own reasons. Sometimes we sniff the same spot, and our noses meet in the search for the perfect scent.

We turn the corner to make the loop. I haven't smelled anything exciting yet, but there has to be something along the way. This walk will be the start of a new beginning for me. I am positive.

I hear a dog barking on the road ahead. My ears perk up, but I realize the bark is muffled. The dog is inside a house. *Bummer.*

Peach is ahead of me, sniffing some flowers. I pass by the flowers in favor of a mailbox post. The post is one of the most popular in the neighborhood. I stop to sniff, but I don't catch anything new or interesting. When I look up, I notice a large gray bunny staring at me from the yard.

This is it!

I look at the bunny rabbit, devising a plan. The bunny is standing on its hind legs next to flowers in a mulch bed not far from me. I should be able to reach it on the leash. The bunny hasn't broken eye contact with me. I sniff the air, but I don't smell a trace of it in the air.

Weird. How is it not giving off a scent?

I don't have too much time, so I make a decision. Using all my pug strength and speed, I lunge at the bunny. I reach it in an instant.

Why hasn't it moved?

I try to stop, but my momentum carries me forward. My head knocks into the hard, not furry, torso of the bunny. The force of the blow sends me reeling backward. I shake my head to regain my bearings. I look at the bunny. It is wobbling a bit. I take a step forward.

"What is Zelda doing?" Lucy asks.

I ignore Lucy and paw at the bunny. The bunny is hard. It still doesn't move. I push harder with my paw. The bunny moves a small amount.

"Zelda, let's go," Hannah says.

This time I use my hard pug head to nudge the bunny. It teeters from side to side. I push it with my paw, and it tumbles to the ground.

"Zelda, what are you doing?" Hannah stomps over to me. She picks up the bunny and sets it right side up. "Let's go home." She pulls me to the sidewalk, but I walk with a gait in my step and a bounce in my tail on the way home.

When we arrive at our house, I notice Nate's car in the driveway.

Nate and Ben are home! I run inside and greet them with many licks and sneezes.

"How was the walk?" Nate asks.

"It was good until Zelda attacked a bunny."

"Wait, what?" Nate asks.

"How did Zelda catch a rabbit on a leash?" Ben asks.

"It wasn't a live bunny. It was a stone bunny in someone's yard. You know, like a yard decoration."

Wait, what?

Nate cracks up with laughter. Ben joins him in the laughter and giggles.

"Only Zelda," Nate says.

I sit on the floor and stare at Hannah and Nate. *Stone bunny? What is that?*

Peach grabs a toy from next to me and shakes it. The toy hits my back. I snap at the toy, grabbing a small portion in my jaw. We play tug-of-war. The tug-of-war game turns into chase, and then into pug sprints.

When I collapse much later in my dog bed, I think about the day. I remember knocking over the bunny. I don't care if it was rock or stone or whatever. I don't know what that means, but I do know that bunny was scared of me. I close my eyes, happy that I finally had a good day of adventure. More days like this one are ahead!

Chapter 9
The Hamburger

Summer is ending, and I am excited for my favorite time of year. I love the cooler temperatures of the autumn season. I love the smells and the leaves, and, of course, the squirrels.

It's been many dark sleeps since I met Squeaks. We lived in a different place then, so I haven't seen him since the move. He was a good friend for the short time we were together. Now I have Peach, but I'd still love to have a squirrel friend!

Peach and I spend most of the day outside with the family. Nate is fighting with something in the garage. Lucy is on her wheels in the driveway. I run with Ben and Peach in the backyard. Hannah sits in a chair in the sun.

When the light starts to fade, Nate emerges from the garage. Hannah brings some goodies outside to the table. Peach and I go to the table to investigate. I leap on the bench and sniff the table. Much to my disappointment, I smell and see no food.

Peach leaves the table to stand by Nate. He opens the lid on this cooking thing. I can't remember what they call this thing, but I know delicious food comes from it. I wait for something to fall. Nate opens the top of the contraption, and a tasty smell flies out of it.

Nate is cooking hamburgers!

I can't get to the hamburger while it's in the cooking thing, so I back away and jump back on the bench of the table. The meat will end up here before eating time. The trick is to get some before my family sits down. Hannah doesn't let me on the table. But if she's not paying attention, I can get onto this outside table. Sometimes Nate doesn't even shoo me off the table if he sees me on it.

I look at the door. Hannah can see me when she walks from the house to the table. It's probably better to stay out of sight. I switch to the bench on the other side of the table. I lie down and keep my tail down. Or at least I try to, but my curly tail bounces from side to side.

I can't help it! It's hamburgers!

The door opens and closes. I hear Hannah place something on the table. When I hear the back door open again, I peer at the table. No meat yet, but some food has appeared. It looks like bread. I like bread, but it's not worth risking my chance at some meat.

I lie on the bench with my eyes closed in my pug stealth position, trying to get as flat as possible so I am not seen. After a few more minutes, Nate opens his cooking thing. I listen closely.

"Peach, what do you think? These hamburgers look good, right?"

I hear the lid close, so I turn my head. Nate walks over to the other side of the table. I hear the small tap of a plate placed on the table.

Now is my chance.

I peak my head above the table. Nate walks inside the house. Ben, Lucy, and Hannah are nowhere to be seen. Peach stares at me from the ground on the other side of the table.

I see the plate of burgers. If I take one quick jump on the table, I can reach the plate. I take one more look in every direction. Then I go for it.

Using my all of my pug grace, I land on the table without making a sound. I take two steps and grab a hamburger in my mouth. I turn to jump down when I see Peach's big eyes.

I take a few swift steps to the edge of the table. I drop the hamburger in front of Peach. She races for it. I return to the plate and grab another in my mouth. I hear the squeak of the door opening. I leap to the bench, then to the ground, and I race into the backyard. Peach follows my lead. We stop running at the back fence and hide behind a tree.

I drop my hamburger on the ground and look to the table. Lucy and Ben are sitting at the table. Hannah and Nate are inside.

Perfect.

I don't waste another moment. The smell of the hamburger is tantalizing. I take a bite. The hamburger is juicy and soft. It melts in my mouth. Before I can stop myself, I gobble up the rest in four big bites. When I finish the last bite, Peach is beside me. She licks my face.

The sound of voices interrupts our moment. I take a few steps closer to listen.

"Nate, are a few more burgers still cooking?"

"No, I took all them off."

"How many did you make?"

"Four."

"Then where are the other two?"

"Huh?"

Nate walks out the back door and looks at the table. He opens the cooking lid, then closes it.

"I swear I made four. Where did they go?"

"I don't know, honey," Hannah says.

"Maybe the dogs ate them," Ben says. All the heads turn to us in the middle of the backyard.

"I don't think so. They have been playing in the back by the fence," Nate says.

That's not true at all. Peach was beside him the whole time he was cooking.

"I'll throw a couple hot dogs on the grill. They only take a few minutes. It will be fine."

"Okay," Hannah says. He hurries inside and comes back. A few minutes later, the family is eating at the table. Peach and I wander to the table and beg for a few bites. Ben sneaks us a few small pieces of hot dog, but it doesn't compare to the whole burgers we just ate.

After dinner, Nate stays outside.

"Zelda, Peach, come!" he shouts. We run to his side. He scratches our heads. "You two are sneaky little thieves. I will let it slide this time. I should know better than to leave food on the table unattended. But next time, I'm not protecting you from Hannah." Peach licks his face.

I don't care if he knows. I ate a whole hamburger and got away with it. This might top outsmarting the greyhound. The one and only pug legend is back!

Chapter 10
The Final Chapter

When I am in need of an adventure, Vacuum is a sure bet to create some chaos and fun. The tough part is that my family won't let me into her closet. I need to wait for her to make an appearance.

While I wait for Vacuum, I keep my nose out for anything mysterious or fun. Peach and I play with our toys and run in the backyard. I bark at dogs walking in front of our house. I snuggle with Lucy at night. The days pass, and I wonder if Vacuum will ever come out to play. I am close to giving up hope that she will come out of her closet when I hear the squeak of a door opening.

I sprint up the stairs. Vacuum's closet door is open! She stares at me from the corner of the bedroom. I bark. Hannah comes into the room.

"Zelda! Leave it!"

No way. I'm not leaving Vacuum today.

I lunge at Vacuum and nip at her.

"Zelda! No!" Hannah shouts. I bark again, so Hannah moves toward me. I run under the bed before she can scoop me into her arms. She sighs. I wait for her to leave, and I plan my next move from the safety of under the bed.

Vacuum rolls to my right. Without a second thought, I dart out from under the bed, barking at her. Hannah grabs me. I squirm, but it's no use. I can't get away. She carries me down the stairs and out the back door. She walks back inside, leaving me in the backyard.

That didn't go well.

A minute later, the door opens. Peach runs outside, but the door closes before I reach it. I wait by the door and look inside. I think Nate is in the kitchen. I bark, but he doesn't come.

I wait by the door, hoping someone will come. I think about when I ripped off Vacuum's arm and left it in the closet at our old house. I remember all the times I chased Vacuum through the house. When Nate finally opens the door, I dash into the house.

The smell in the house stops me cold. The smell is different than Vacuum's usual odor. Something isn't right with her or the house. I run up the stairs and look for Vacuum. I look through the crack in the door of her closet. She isn't there, but the smell is everywhere. My nose does all the work. The more I sniff, the more the smell reminds me of one similar to the bright light that burns in the backyard at night.

What happened?

I have a mystery on my paws. It's time to get to work. I search for clues in the house, but I can't find anything to indicate what happened to Vacuum or where she went. I can't solve the mystery without clues. I have to keep my pug eyes, ears, and nose ready to figure out what happened to her.

Peach and I go outside as the light begins to fade. I sniff the corners of the fence and look for rogue squirrels or birds. When Nate calls us inside, I trot to the door. As I trot, I catch a glint of teal and blue from the side of the house.

Wait a minute.

I veer off course from the door to the corner of the yard along the fence and driveway. On the other side of the giant brown can, I see Vacuum. I can't see her entire body, but she is there.

What is she doing outside?

"Zelda! Let's go! Inside!" Nate shouts.

I have to go inside. Figures. I was getting close to figuring it all out. Tomorrow, I will find the reason Vacuum is outside and figure out what to do.

I sprint inside. Peach is already in the living room chewing on a nylabone. Nate closes the door behind me. I run into the living room and jump on the couch next to Ben.

I wake up the next morning ready to solve the mystery. I don't bother waking Peach. I need to do this alone. I run down the stairs to the back door. Hannah lets me outside.

There is a chill in the air, but the sun is beaming down on the grass. It's going to be a great day. I walk to the corner to get a better look at Vacuum. *She's not there!*

I blink a few times. Vacuum isn't there. Did I imagine it last night? I look again, and I realize that the big brown box is gone too. Where did they go?

I circle the backyard, but I can't see anything or smell any clues. Defeated, I limp my way to the back door. I go inside and plop on the couch.

The noise of a big truck awakens me from my morning nap. I recognize the noise. The trucks come and stop in front of our house for a moment. They empty the big brown box and continue down the street.

Wait a second! Why didn't I think of this before?

I jump to my perch on top of the couch and look out the front window. The big brown box rests on the edge of the driveway. Vacuum sits beside the box. The trucks are one house away. I watch the truck stop in front of our driveway. It dumps the brown box in the back of the truck. Then a man takes Vacuum and throws her in the back of the truck. The truck drives to the next house.

Once something goes in that truck, it never comes back.

I can't believe it. Vacuum is gone. After all this time, I dreamed of her leaving the house, but now that it has actually happened, I don't know what to think. She isn't coming back. My arch nemesis is gone.

I drop down to the floor and curl up in my dog bed. I can't think about this anymore. I close my eyes, pushing the thoughts of Vacuum away.

I mope throughout the house the next day. I am in shock about what happened to Vacuum.

Hannah spent quite a bit of time with Vacuum. Why would she throw Vacuum away? Something must have happened–maybe a falling out? I bet it has to do with the smell from the last time Vacuum came out. That has to be the reason.

For the rest of the day, I stay glued to Hannah's side. I sit on her lap while she stares at the big screen. I follow her into the kitchen and clean up scraps on the floor while she cooks. I bring her a toy after dinner. We play tug-of-war until I grow tired. Then I curl up next to her on the couch again. This time I give her face a quick kiss before closing my eyes.

"Aww, thank you, Zelda," she says after I give her the kiss. She likes the attention that I gave her all day. I'm glad. I don't want to end up like Vacuum.

The next day is uneventful, so when I wake after the next dark sleep, my worries and sadness are gone. I am back to my spunky pug nature, looking for adventure everywhere I go.

Peach and I go for a walk with Hannah and Lucy in the afternoon. Hannah has my leash, so I don't have an opportunity to break free or lead the way. I don't mind. I love the fresh air and the cool breeze. The leaves are falling through the sky. I know leaf piles will appear soon. I can't wait to run and jump through leaf piles again.

When I return home, Nate is in the living room with a big box. He leaves the room. I walk to the box and sniff, but I don't recognize the smell. The box is too tall for me to look into, so I jump on the couch and wait.

Nate returns a few minutes later. He opens the box and pulls out a few parts of something. He snaps the parts together in a few minutes. When he is finished, I can't believe my eyes.

Vacuum is back.

But it's not Vacuum. It looks similar to her, but there are a few differences. Her colors are different. She has no smell and hasn't made any noise. But if this Vacuum is anything like the other Vacuum, that doesn't mean anything.

I stare at Vacuum.

Is it her?

It can't be her, right? I have to know for sure. Nate pulls a black rope from Vacuum. I wait, knowing what is coming next, even though I won't like it.

A noise fills the room. The noise reminds me of her, but it is a little quieter. Nate pushes Vacuum across the rug, and then the noise stops. I approach Vacuum and sniff. She doesn't do anything. She doesn't make noise or move. Her smell is different.

It's not her.

I'm not sure if I'm relieved or upset that Vacuum is gone forever. I know it for sure now.

Hannah walks into the room. "Everything okay with the new vacuum?" she asks.

"Yep. Zelda didn't even bark at it."

"Really?" Nate nods.

"Did you want me to vacuum upstairs?" Nate asks.

"Only if you want to."

"Does anybody ever want to vacuum?" Hannah shakes her head. Nate laughs.

He picks up Vacuum and carries her upstairs. I follow him into Lucy's room. A few minutes later the noise returns. I jump on Lucy's bed and watch Nate and Vacuum move together.

After a few minutes, I can't stand it anymore. I jump off the bed and chase Vacuum, barking at her. They move into Ben's room. I am right behind them. Nate shouts at me.

Peach joins the fun, and we are barking, biting, and chasing Vacuum. It's a riot. I love it.

When Vacuum stops roaring, our tongues are hanging out. I am tired in the best possible way. Vacuum goes in the closet. I bark at her and then go downstairs. I take a few sips from my water bowl and then collapse on the couch.

Nate comes down the stairs a few minutes later.

"It sounds like the new vacuum has the same effect on Zelda."

It is a new Vacuum. I was right.

"Yeah. I thought maybe since it was quieter, the dogs wouldn't bark, but I was wrong," Nate says.

"Yep. Zelda still hates the vacuum."

"And we love her anyway," Nate says.

"Yep, we do," Hannah replies.

With Hannah and Nate's words, I jump off the couch. I stand on my hind legs and lick Nate's hands. Then I run over to Hannah. She scoops me into her arms. I lick her cheek. *I am not Vacuum. I can never be replaced.*

Hannah and Nate's words reverberate through my pug brain for the next several days. I think about what's happened this summer–the creek, the cone, the rain, and the rabbit. I think about my favorite times since I moved in with my family. I made friends with Squeaks the squirrel. I was chased by a goose. My family adopted Peach so I could have a sister. I went to the beach. I even went on a canoe trip. It's been an incredible ride. Sometimes I go through rough patches, but for the first time, I realize that's okay. As long as I am with my family, the adventures will never stop, and I will always have them by my side. With that in mind, I look forward to the days ahead as the one and only Zelda pug.

A NOTE FROM THE AUTHOR

When I speak to classrooms filled with students, I am often asked how and why I started writing the Zelda books. I love answering that question because the Zelda books were never "supposed" to be anything more than a few funny short stories that I wrote to practice my craft. But, after writing a few stories based loosely off the antics of my real life Zelda, I couldn't stop writing. The stories flowed through my fingers on to the keyboard. Soon after, *The Adventures of Zelda: A Pug Tale* was published.

The early reader response was better than expected. I kept writing and by book three, it was clear that young readers enjoyed reading about a stubborn, adventurous pug.

The most rewarding part for me are the messages and emails I receive from parents thanking me for writing a book that their son or daughter wants to read. I know the Zelda books aren't for every kid, but I'm glad that some kids discover their love of reading from the series.

Five books into the series, I have decided to give Zelda (and Peach) an indefinite break to focus on a few other writing projects. With all of her success, Zelda is becoming a bit of a diva, so she needs some time off to get back to her normal pug life.

While Zelda enjoys some time off, I am writing a new kids' book series in the next year, along with continuing to write young adult fiction. At this point, I don't know when I will return to writing in the Zelda Pug series. However, we are all very thankful for the support from our fans so far. Thank you!

Zelda, Peach, Brian, and I

AFTERWORD

Thank you for choosing to spend your time with a book. I couldn't do this without you.

Reviews are a huge encouragement to authors. If you have a few minutes, head over to Amazon, Goodreads or your favorite online retailer and write a few sentences about the book. If you want to know when my next book is coming out and receive a free PDF copy of Batpeach, sign up for my email list.

Thank you to my editor, Candace Johnson, for always fitting Zelda into her schedule. Thanks to Michael McFarland for his amazing artwork.

Thanks to my mom, dad, stepdad, sister, and my extended family and friends for their constant encouragement.

Thanks to the real Zelda and Peach for allowing me to write stories about them.

Brian, I couldn't do this without your support. I love you.

John 14:12

ABOUT THE AUTHOR

Author Kristen Otte writes books for children, teens, and adults. Her mission is to bring joy and laughter through stories to people young and old. When she isn't writing or reading, you may find her on the basketball court coaching her high school girls' team. If she isn't writing or coaching, she is probably chasing her husband and dogs around the house.

BOOKS BY KRISTEN OTTE

The Adventures of Zelda: A Pug Tale
The Adventures of Zelda: The Second Saga
The Adventures of Zelda: Pug and Peach
The Adventures of Zelda: The Four Seasons
The Adventures of Zelda: The One and Only Pug
The Perfect Smile (Eastbrook 0.5)
The Photograph (Eastbrook 1)
The Evolution of Lillie Gable (Eastbrook 2)

Learn more about Kristen, her books, and her workshops at her website: www.kristenotte.com.